Dear Parents and Teachers,

In an easy-reader format, **My Readers** introduce classic stories to children who are learning to read. Although favorite characters and time-tested tales are the basis for **My Readers**, the books tell completely new stories and are freshly and beautifully illustrated.

My Readers are available in three levels:

1 **Level One** is for the emergent reader and features repetitive language and word clues in the illustrations.

2 **Level Two** is for more advanced readers who still need support saying and understanding some words. Stories are longer with word clues in the illustrations.

3 **Level Three** is for independent, fluent readers who enjoy working out occasional unfamiliar words. The stories are longer and divided into chapters.

Encourage children to select books based on interests, not reading levels. Read aloud with children, showing them how to use the illustrations for clues. With adult guidance and rereading, children will eventually read the desired book on their own.

Here are some ways you might want to use this book with children:

- Talk about the title and the cover illustrations. Encourage the child to use these to predict what the story is about.
- Discuss the interior illustrations and try to piece together a story based on the pictures. Does the child want to change or adjust his first prediction?
- After children reread a story, suggest they retell or act out a favorite part.

My Readers will not only help children become readers, they will serve as an introduction to some of the finest classic children's books available today.

—LAURA ROBB
Educator and Reading Consultant

For activities and reading tips, visit myreadersonline.com

For Zubiaga, whose bright spirit
will never be forgotten by those who knew him

SQUARE
FISH
An Imprint of Macmillan

Library of Congress Cataloging-in-Publication Data
Day, Alexandra.
Carl and the kitten / story and pictures by Alexandra Day. — 1st ed.
    p.   cm.
Summary: Carl helps a little kitten that is stuck in a tree.
[1. Helpfulness—Fiction. 2. Dogs—Fiction. 3. Cats—Fiction.] I. Title.
PZ7.D32915Can 2011 [E]—dc22 2011001448
ISBN 978-0-312-68196-8 (hardcover): 10 9 8 7 6 5 4 3 2
ISBN 978-0-312-68197-5 (paperback): 10 9 8 7 6 5 4 3

Book design by Patrick Collins/Véronique Lefèvre Sweet

Square Fish logo designed by Filomena Tuosto

First Edition: 2011

myreadersonline.com
mackids.com

This is a Level 1 book

Lexile: 230L

CARL and the KITTEN

story and pictures by
Alexandra Day

SQUARE
FISH

Macmillan Children's Publishing Group
New York

One of Carl's friends
needs help.
Who can it be?

It's Mama Cat.

One of her kittens
ran away . . .

and climbed a tree.
It was easy
to climb up.

It is not so easy
to climb down.

"Jump," says Carl.
"I will catch you."

Meow!

Kitten is afraid to jump.

"Walk down
the branch,"
says Carl,

"and jump on my back."

Kitten steps out
on the branch.

Meow!

Kitten is still afraid to jump.

"Wait!" says Carl.

"I can help you."

"Now jump, Kitten," says Carl.
"It's not so far."
Meow!

"Is this better, Kitten?"
asks Carl.
Meow!

"I'm much closer now,"
says Carl.
Meow!

"Jump, Kitten.
You can do it."

Uh-oh!

Kitten is safe!

"Let's go see Mama Cat,"
says Carl.